Copyright © 2001 by Michael Neugebauer Verlag,
an imprint of Nord-Süd Verlag AG, Gossau Zürich, Switzerland
First published in Switzerland under the title Wenn der wilde Wombat kommt
English translation © 2002 by North-South Books Inc., New York

First published in the United States, Great Britain, Canada,
Australia, and New Zealand in 2002 by North-South Books,
an imprint of Nord-Süd Verlag AG, Gossau Zürich, Switzerland.

Distributed in the United States by North-South Books Inc., New York.

Library of Congress Cataloging-in-Publication Data is available.
A CIP catalogue record for this book is available from The British Library.
ISBN 0-7358-1511-9 (trade edition) 10 9 8 7 6 5 4 3 2 1
ISBN 0-7358-1512-7 (library edition) 10 9 8 7 6 5 4 3 2 1

For more information about our books, and the authors and artists
who create them, visit our web site: www.northsouth.com

Printed in Italy

THE WILD WOMBAT

BY UDO WEIGELT
ILLUSTRATED BY ANNE-KATRIN PIEPENBRINK

TRANSLATED BY KATHRYN GRELL

A MICHAEL NEUGEBAUER BOOK
NORTH-SOUTH BOOKS
NEW YORK/LONDON

On a bright summer day at the zoo, a parrot heard one zookeeper say to another, "Today the wild wombat is coming—all the way from Australia! We must be very careful with him."

The parrot flew to the baby seal and told him about the wild wombat. "Do you think that the zookeeper is really afraid of the wild wombat?" asked the baby seal.

"It sounded like that," said the parrot. "The zookeeper said they must be very careful with him!"

Frightened, the seal swam to shore
to warn the chameleon.
When the chameleon heard about the wild
wombat, he gasped in terror.
If the seal is so afraid, thought the chameleon,
then the wild wombat must be a dreadful
sea monster that can swim faster than any seal.

The chameleon hurried over to tell the owl about the wild wombat.

The owl trembled in fear. If the chameleon is so afraid, thought the owl, then the wild wombat must be an awful creature that can hide himself better than any chameleon and then jump out and frighten everyone.

The owl told the terrible news about the wild wombat
to the tortoise, who rushed over to warn the gazelle.
"The wild wombat is coming!" the tortoise said. "He is a terrible monster
with enormous wings and sharp teeth! He hides himself better than
a chameleon and can swim faster than a seal!"
Frightened, the gazelle ran to the elephant.

"Watch out!" she called to the elephant. "The wild wombat is coming! He has a stronger shell than a tortoise. He has fangs and claws. He can fly and make himself invisible like a chameleon. He can swim faster than a seal, and he comes all the way from Australia!"

If the gazelle is so afraid, thought the elephant, then the wild wombat must be a horrible beast indeed that can surely run faster than the swiftest gazelle. Immediately, he told the kangaroo all about the wild wombat.

A pair of flamingos overheard the kangaroo's story and ran to the lion as fast as they could. "The wild wombat is coming!" they called. "He is bigger than an elephant and can run faster than a gazelle! He has a shell like a tortoise and enormous wings and sharp talons like an owl. He can make himself invisible better than a chameleon and swims faster than a seal! Worst of all, the kangaroo says he devoured his home and all the animals in it!"

When he heard this, even the brave lion felt afraid.

The terrified animals all rushed off to hide from the wild wombat.
None of the visitors could find a single animal at the zoo.

Then a van drove into the zoo with a big crate.

A pair of zookeepers unloaded the crate in a pen in the middle of the zoo. It was time! The door of the crate was opened. A brown animal peered out. Then slowly he emerged from the crate and looked around curiously.

"I am a wombat, and I have come here to live with you."

But none of the animals dared to leave their hiding places.

The wild wombat was confused.

Finally, the parrot flew over. "Hello! Are you the wild wombat?" he asked.

"Yes, of course," said the wombat. "Are you the only other animal in the zoo?"

The parrot looked around. Where *were* the other animals? "This is very strange," said the parrot. "I'm sure I mentioned that you were coming. I can't imagine why they aren't here. . . ."

WOMBAT

Like the kangaroo, the wombat is a marsupial and is native to Australia. It can grow to be thirty-nine inches long. It looks like a small bear and lives in underground tunnels that it digs itself. The wombat is nocturnal. It eats roots, mushrooms, grasses, and herbs. The wombat is a good-natured and peaceful animal that can live for up to twenty years. Unfortunately, the wombat is one of Australia's most endangered species.

Wombat